My Name Was Hussein

By
Hristo Kyuchukov

Illustrated by
Allan Eitzen

Boyds Mills Press

Published by Boyds Mills Press, Inc.
A Highlights Company
815 Church Street
Honesdale, Pennsylvania 18431
Printed in China

Publisher Cataloging-in-Publication Data (U.S.)

Kryuchukov, Hristo.
My name was Hussein / by Hristo Kyuchukov ; illustrated by Allan Eitzen.—1st ed.
[32] p. : col. ill. ; cm.
Summary: When an army invades a village, a Muslim boy and his family are forced to take Christian names.
ISBN 1-56397-964-0
1. Islam — Juvenile fiction. 2. Muslims — Juvenile fiction. (1. Islam — Fiction. 2. Muslims — Fiction.) I. Eitzen, Allan. II. Title.
[E] 21 PZ7.K798Mn 2004
2003112228

First edition, 2004
The text is set in 13-point Caxton Book.
The illustrations are done in pen and ink and watercolor.

Visit our Web site at www.boydsmillspress.com

10 9 8 7 6 5 4 3 2 1

Note: *Some customs may vary among members of the same religion in different parts of the world. In the Roma society depicted in this book, for instance, the playing of stringed instruments and the manner in which Muslim women wear scarves are considered acceptable practices.*

To the memory of my parents
—H. K.

Dedicated to peace for families everywhere
—A. E.

My name was Hussein.
I was born in this village.
I belong to a Roma family.
Some call us Gypsies,
but we are the Roma people.
Our people came to Bulgaria
many years ago from a place
called India.

In our family, we are Muslims.
That is our religion.
We celebrate many holidays.
For every holiday, my mother cooks
beautiful foods for us to eat.
Our house smells delicious.
I love the smells.
During holidays, our friends
and relatives visit us.

We observe Ramadan.
For a month, my parents do not
eat during the day.
During this time, they pray
extra prayers.
At night, we eat a special meal
called *iftar*.

The last day of Ramadan is the best.
My father goes to the mosque.
When he comes back,
he gives us candies.
My little brother and I kiss our
parents' hands to say thank you.

We also visit my grandparents on holidays.
I love my grandparents.
They are happy when they see me.
They hug me and hold me on their laps.
They give me candies that smell nice, like roses.
My grandmother cooks puddings made of rice and nuts.
She knows exactly what I like to eat.

Before each holiday, my mother and
grandmother paint their hands.
They put henna color on their palms and fingers.
They wear special clothes.
This is to show that the holiday has started.

My father buys new shirts for me and my little brother.
He buys new pants and shoes for us.
We have good clothes for the holidays.

I love my name Hussein.
In Arabic, it means handsome.
My grandfather was named Hussein.
His grandfather was also named Hussein.
I am proud of my name.
Even so, everyone in my family
calls me Hughsy.
It is their special name for me.

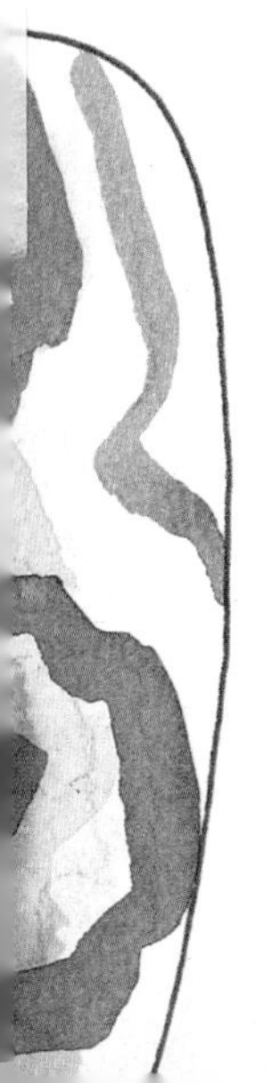

I live in the middle of a loving family.
I have many aunts and uncles and cousins.
We enjoy happy times together.

Then one day everything changed.
The army came with tanks,
cannons, guns, and dogs.

No one was allowed to leave the village.
We could not visit our relatives.
We could not go outside at night.
We could not speak our Romani language in the streets.

It was Ramadan.
I wanted to visit my grandparents.
I wanted to taste my grandmother's puddings.
My mother would not let me go.
She was afraid of the soldiers.

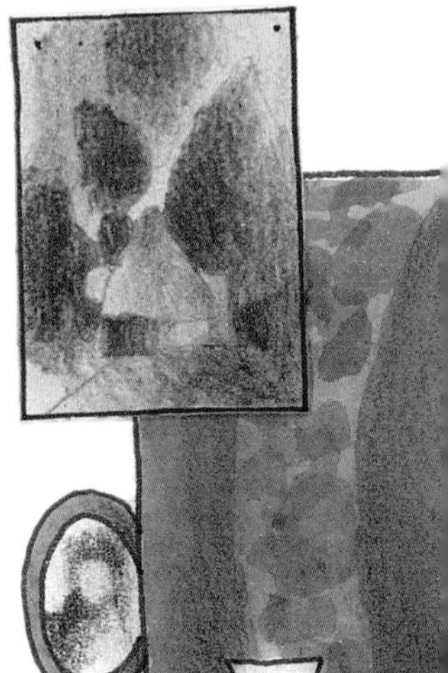

On the first day of Ramadan,
the men go to the mosque.
I went with my father,
but the mosque was closed.

The soldiers did not let us inside to pray.
They stood in front of the doors.
We had to go back home.

My father could not buy us
new shirts for Ramadan.
He was not allowed to go to the shops.
My little brother was crying.
He wanted a new shirt.
He wanted to see our grandparents.
I did, too.

My father sat in a chair by the window.
He did not speak to me.
He would not play with me.
I did not understand why.

Then soldiers came to our house.
They had guns. They had dogs.
I was so scared. They ordered us to
report to the mayor's office.
Why? I wondered. What did we do?

We did as we were told.
A policeman in the office tore my parents'
identity cards into little pieces.
"You must change your names," he said.
"You must choose Christian names.
Come back with new names
and you will get new identity cards."

My father's name was Selim.
He did not want another name.
My mother's name was Sanie.
She did not want another name.
My brother's name was Hassan.
He did not want another name.
And I did not want another name.

On our way home, my father said,
“I am not a Christian. I do not want a Christian name.”
My mother said, “We have no choice.
We need our identity cards.”

Now I have a new identity card, too.
It says my name is Harry.
At school, my teachers call me Harry.
On the streets, my parents call me Harry.
But at home, my parents still call me Hughsy.
What would you call me?
My name was Hussein.

AUTHOR'S NOTE

Bulgaria is located in southeastern Europe, between Romania and Turkey. Today, it is a democracy. But it wasn't always so. After the Second World War, Bulgaria fell under the rule of communists, who determined that the country should include only ethnic Bulgarians. Minorities were persecuted. In the middle of the 1980s, the government launched a radical plan to change the identities of those who were not ethnic Bulgarians. Over the course of a few weeks, more than one million Muslims, including Roma, Turks, and other minorities, were forced to choose Christian names. It happened to me. This story is based on events in my life. Until I was twenty-two years old, my name was Hussein.

— H. K.